ROBLOX
ULTIMATE AVATAR
STICKER BOOK

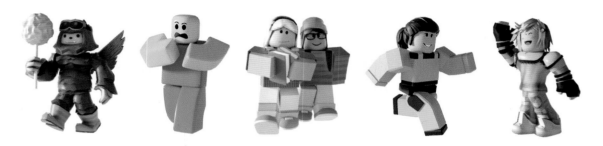

HARPER FESTIVAL
An Imprint of HarperCollinsPublishers

Roblox High School developed by Cindering
Miner's Haven developed by berezaa Games
Speed Run 4 developed by Vurse
Jailbreak developed by Badimo
Work at a Pizza Place developed by Dued1
Neverland Lagoon developed by SelDraken & Teiyia
Skybound 2 developed by Imaginaerum
Theme Park Tycoon 2 developed by Den_S
Zombie Rush developed by Beacon Studio
MeepCity developed by Alexnewtron
Design It! developed by tktech

Original English language edition first published in 2019 by Egmont UK Limited,
The Yellow Building, 1 Nicholas Road, London, W11 4AN, United Kingdom.

Written by Craig Jelley
Designed by Andrea Philpots
Special thanks to the entire Roblox team

ISBN 978-0-06-286268-6
❖
19 20 21 22 23 RTLO 10 9 8 7 6 5 4 3 2 1
First US Edition

HALLWAY RUSH

■ ROBLOX HIGH SCHOOL

The bell rings for the start of the day at Roblox High School, and eager students are still filing into their classrooms. Create an avatar to send to class, and add in some extra stickers to liven up the school.

UNDERGROUND MINES

You've restored an abandoned subterranean base to its former glory, but there are still some improvements to be made. Use your stickers to add in more machinery and max out your avatar's mining skills.

CASTLE SIEGE

■ **CASTLE STUDIO TEMPLATE**

The kingdoms of Korblox and Redcliff are engaged in combat outside a Redcliff bastion. Who will be victorious? Add stickers of fearless knights and their weapons to turn the tide of the battle.

OBBY COURSE

■ SPEED RUN 4

Run, hop, or jump your way around this obby – just don't look down. Get your avatar ready for action in awesome parkour gear, and fill this obby with hazards to maximize the challenge.

PRISON COURTYARD

■ JAILBREAK

The prisoners are trying to break out of jail, and it's only a matter of time before they succeed. Will your avatar become one of the escapee inmates? Or deploy in SWAT gear to quash the breakout?

PIRATE COVE

■ NEVERLAND LAGOON

You've splashed down into the icy waters of Neverland Lagoon. Will you choose the pirate's life for your avatar, or go swimming under the surface with the mermaids?

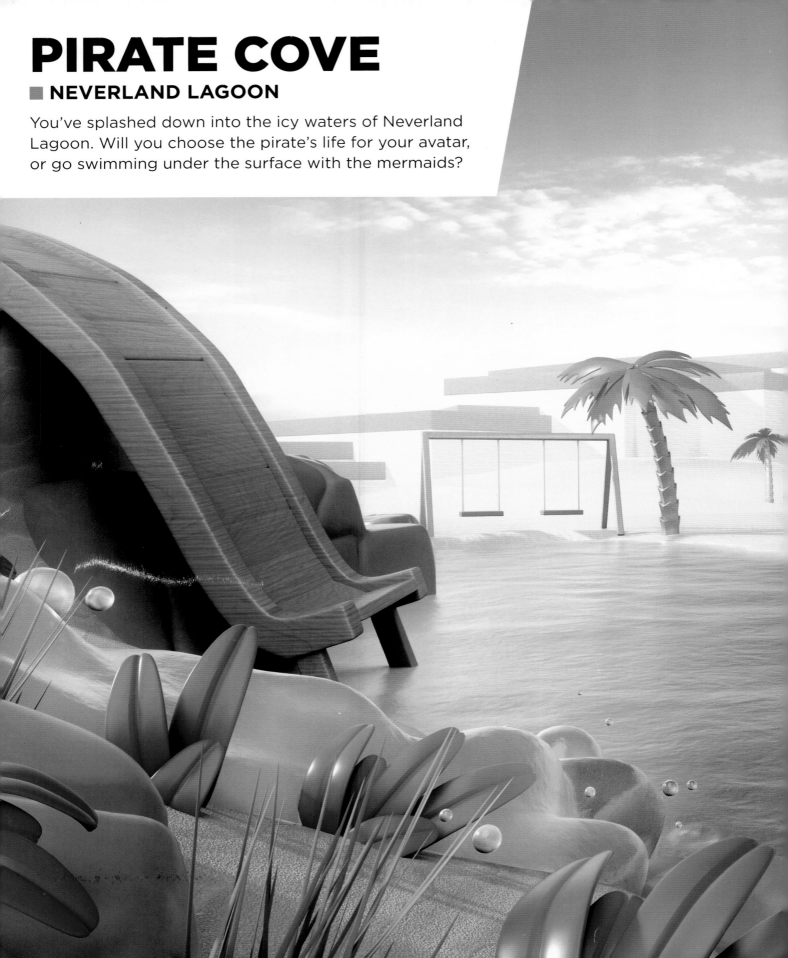

FLOATING ISLANDS

■ **SKYBOUND 2**

Ready, aim, fire the cannonballs! An aerial encounter has erupted high above the floating islands. Get your avatar ready for battle, then fill the scene with gravity-defying flying machines.

FUN FAIR

■ **THEME PARK TYCOON 2**

What better way to spend the evening than at an awesome theme park full of exhilarating rides? Add in some excited visitors, then get your avatar ready for all the fun of the fair!

NOOB

ZOMBIE HORDES

■ ZOMBIE RUSH

You thought you were safe underground, but you couldn't have been more wrong! Equip your avatar with gear to give it a fighting chance of escaping the zombie-infested caverns.

PLAZA PARTY

■ **MEEPCITY**

Night is falling over Robloxia, and the residents are flocking to MeepCity for a party in the plaza! Get the celebration started with some super-fun gear, then deck out your avatar in perfect party style.

ULTIMATE AVATAR

■ DESIGN IT!

How does your avatar stack up against everyone else's? Let your imagination run wild and create the ultimate avatar that will stand proudly on the top spot of the Design It! podium.